JOHN DEERE

This is My Book

Name _____

Date _____

Printed by TOMY International, Inc.
with permission of Deere & Company.

2012

ISBN 1-887327-19-3

JOHNNY TRACTOR AND FRIENDS

TAKING OVER

A JOHN DEERE STORYBOOK FOR LITTLE FOLKS

From a Story by T.J. Cahill

Illustrated by Kirk Barron

Late one night Peter Pickup was in the shed talking with Corey Combine. "Corey," he said, "there sure was a lot of excitement at the house today, I wonder what is going on?"

"Well," said Corey, "I heard Farmer Fowler say somebody new was coming and he was going to take over."

Corey was one of the biggest and hardest workers on the farm but sometimes he wasn't the best listener. "Take over what?" asked Peter. "Take over the farm?" he thought out loud. "That must be it, someone is coming to take over the farm!" Peter was a proud pickup with a great imagination that sometimes got him into trouble.

"But Peter," said Corey, "Farmer Fowler just started his job on the farm." Young Tad Fowler was all grown up now and had just taken over the farm from his father Bob. "It doesn't make sense that someone else would take over the farm. He is such a good farmer, and he takes good care of us."

"He must not be good enough," said Peter. "He is just too young to do the job." Corey did not like the sound of someone else running him in the field. "I like Farmer Fowler, he is nice. What if the new person isn't as nice...or worse...he sells us?" said Corey, with a worried look on his face.

"Well, he won't sell me," said Peter, "I am too new to sell, and besides, Farmer Fowler will probably take me with him."

This made Corey feel very sad. That was the end of the conversation for the night.

The next morning was bright and sunny, but that did not make Corey feel any better.

The big shed door slid open, and Farmer Fowler came in and drove off in Peter.

"Oh, it must be true," said Corey to himself, "Peter is going with Farmer Fowler and I'm going to be sold." Corey was sure he was going to be sold to a strange farmer who would not take care of him.

Later that morning Peter came back, but he did not say a word to Corey. Corey was just about to ask Peter where he had gone, when a great big, brand-new, shiny green tractor came into the shed.
"Hi", said the big new tractor, "My name is Johnny, I'm going to take over the fieldwork for Farmer Fowler."

"Well, that's the last time I will listen to you," said Corey to Peter. "Well, you are the one that said someone was coming to take over," Peter snapped back.

"WHAT ARE YOU TALKING ABOUT?" Johnny said in his deep commanding voice. Peter and Corey stopped their arguing and explained the whole story to Johnny.

"I am not here to *take over*, but only to help Farmer Fowler with the fieldwork," said Johnny. "I will pull the big disk in the spring to get the fields ready for planting, and then pull the planter and do the cultivating,"

Johnny continued. "I'll pull the wagons filled with grain, and then work the fields again after the harvest. But I can't take over the whole farm."

"Farmer Fowler will need your help, too." Peter and Corey were ashamed of how they got the story all mixed up. "It looks like you both learned a lesson," said Johnny. "The next time make sure you have all the facts, and don't let your imaginations *take over*. Let's get going!"